WITHDRAWN

Simply Science

COMMUNICATION

Discover Science Through Facts and Fun

By Gerry Bailey and Steve Way

Science and curriculum consultant:
Debra Voege, M.A., science curriculum resource teacher

Gareth Stevens
Publishing

Please visit our web site at www.garethstevens.com.
For a free catalog describing our list of high-quality books, call 1-800-542-2595 (USA)
or 1-800-387-3178 (Canada). Our fax: 1-877-542-2596

Library of Congress Cataloging-in-Publication Data

Bailey, Gerry.
　　　　Communication/by Gerry Bailey.
　　　　　　p. cm.—(Simply Science)
　　　　Includes bibliographical references and index.
　　　　ISBN-10: 0-8368-9226-7　ISBN-13: 978-0-8368-9226-0 (lib. bdg.)
　　　　1. Telecommunication—Juvenile literature.　2. Mass media—Juvenile literature.
　　　　I. Title.
　　TK5102.4.B34　2009
　　384—dc22　　　　　　　　　　　　　　　　　　　　　　　　　　2008012376

This North American edition first published in 2009 by
Gareth Stevens Publishing
A Weekly Reader® Company
1 Reader's Digest Road
Pleasantville, NY 10570-7000 USA

Gareth Stevens Senior Managing Editor: Lisa M. Herrington
Gareth Stevens Creative Director: Lisa Donovan
Gareth Stevens Designer: Keith Plechaty
Gareth Stevens Associate Editor: Amanda Hudson
Special thanks to Mark Sachner

Photo Credits: Cover (tc) Soundsnaps/Shutterstock Inc., (bl) Roman Milert/Shutterstock Inc.;
p. 5 Keren Su/Corbis; p. 10 The British Library, all rights reserved; p. 12 (t) Gianni Tortolli/Science Photo
Library; (b) West Semitic Research/Dead Sea Scrolls Foundation/ Corbis; p. 13 (l) British Library/AKG-
Images, (tr) John Hedgecoe/TopFoto, (br) Randy Faris/Corbis; p.17 Newton Page/Shutterstock Inc.;
p. 18 Bettmann/Corbis; p. 21 (tl) Soundsnaps/Shutterstock Inc., (bl) R. Gino Santa Maria/Shutterstock
Inc., (bc) Lance Bellers/Shutterstock Inc., (br) Pure Digital 2006; pp. 22–23 Telepix/Alamy.; p. 24 Roman
Milert/Shutterstock; p. 25 Chris Cheadle/Stone/Getty Images; p. 26 Alejandro Bolivar/EPA/Corbis;
p. 27 Skyscan/ Science Photo Library.

Illustrations: Steve Boulter and Xact Studio, Diagrams: Ralph Pitchford

Printed in the United States of America

1 2 3 4 5 6 7 8 9 10 09 08

Simply Science
COMMUNICATION

Contents

Let's Communicate!

When you laugh, you tell people you're happy. You can write a message to tell someone where you're going. When you read a book, watch television, or go to the movies, someone else is telling you things. All of this is communication. It's about sharing thoughts and ideas!

Communication is:

... phoning a friend

... reading a book

... **discussing a great movie**

... sending an e-mail

... **or just showing people how you feel.**

A group of Chinese children sing.

Making Sounds

When you learn a language, you hear and learn lots of sounds. Each sound has a different meaning, and you must learn each meaning.

Talking to Someone

When you talk, a part your throat, called your voice box, vibrates. It makes the air around it move as well.

The moving air travels in waves, called **sound waves**. Sound waves come out of your mouth and move through the air.

Sound waves are picked up by the sensitive part of the ears. They make this part of the ear vibrate. The brain decides what the vibrations mean.

Waves in the Air?

Sound waves are created when something vibrates. It could be your throat or a musical instrument.

Tiny air particles around the source of the vibration begin to move. The air particles are squashed together by the vibration. This is called "compression."

The compression moves outward. Air particles are then pulled apart as the sound wave moves along. This is called "rarefaction."

When the wave **sequence** of compressions and rarefactions reaches your ear, you hear the sound!

Learning Sounds

The first people probably communicated with each other using simple sounds. Some sounds came to be understood as meaning certain things. "Ugh" might mean "hello!" or it might mean "there's a big mastodon chasing you." So it was important to learn just what a sound meant!

Language

Over a long period of time, more and more sounds were given special meanings. Soon groups of people were speaking a language of sounds. That's what language is: a whole lot of sounds that mean something to a group of people.

Not understanding each other can lead to disaster!

Unfortunately, different people in different places use different sounds. So if we want to understand them, we have to learn their special sounds, too.

Papyrus Letters

Papyrus is a water plant that grows in Egypt. The ancient Egyptians used strips of fiber from its stem to make a kind of paper. This was one of the first kinds of paper ever invented.

Clay tablets are too heavy to mail.

A Plant to Write on

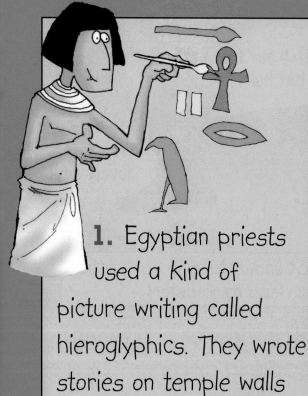

1. Egyptian priests used a Kind of picture writing called hieroglyphics. They wrote stories on temple walls or marked messages into pieces of clay.

2. Clay is heavy! They needed a lightweight material to carry messages to people.

Papyrus Scrolls

Papyrus sheets were rolled into **scrolls** and tied with a leather strap. The library at Alexandria in ancient Egypt held more than 400,000 papyrus scrolls.

Hieroglyphic writing used symbols to form messages.

3. It is likely that someone tried writing on papyrus leaf. It was light, but not very strong.

4. Then someone realized that a very thin, woven mat of papyrus would make a great writing material.

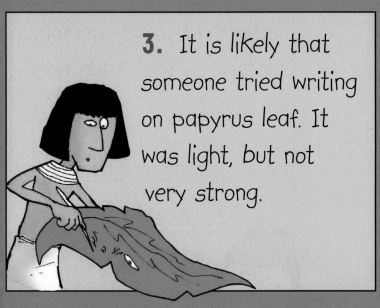

5. Strips of papyrus fiber were pressed together and then cut into long sheets. The papyrus was rolled up and sent around the country bearing written messages.

Printing Blocks

A printing block is a block of wood, or some other material, on which a letter has been carved, or engraved.

Long ago, Chinese officials used stone blocks to make wax seals to close important documents. This led to the invention of engraved wooden blocks that could be used to print documents such as religious scrolls.

A Block of Letters

1. Copying documents took a lot of time and patience. Each letter had to be carefully written so that each was an exact copy of the previous one.

2. Making each letter took a long time. There had to be a way of making lots of copies at once.

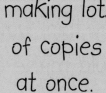

3. But when ink was spread on the carving, and it was placed face down on paper, it printed the wrong way. All the letters and words were backward!

Perhaps the characters could be carved into a **mold** instead.

4. The answer was to print the letters onto fine paper first, and paste this front side down onto the block before carving. In this way, the letters would be engraved backward. Then they would print the right way.

The Story of Books

The first books weren't really books at all. They were smooth tablets made of soft clay that people could write on.

Later, **scribes** used lengths of papyrus made from plants or parchment made from animal skin. These could be rolled up into scrolls.

Finally, someone came up with the idea of cutting the scrolls into pieces and making pages. The book was born!

Tablets

The first books, or tablets, were probably used to record what merchants bought and sold. They were used as a **bookkeeping** tool.

Scrolls

Later, scrolls were used to list laws and to write down religious beliefs.

The Codex

An early kind of book with a cover and pages was first used more than 2,000 years ago.

The pages were stitched together. This early form of book was called a codex. Later, the printing press was invented.

On Press

Early printing press books were often bound in leather. Modern books can be bound in board as "hardbacks" or in paper as "paperbacks."

The Printing Press

Look! I've made the first printed book!

The printing press is a machine that can print whole pages of a book at once. Before the press, books were written by hand. This invention made books available to many more people.

A Press to Print Books

1. Johannes Gutenberg was trained as a goldsmith. But he was also a printer. He wanted to invent a machine that would make printing much quicker, so books could be read by more people.

2. Copying books by hand took a long time. **Scribes** took ages decorating them.

Blocks of Type

Type was made on blocks. A separate letter was on each block, and the blocks could then be laid out in even lines of type. These were held together in a flat box called a bed.

The bed of type was then placed in a printing press with ink spread on it and pressed down to print a page.

3. The Chinese and Koreans printed with wood blocks. Each letter had to be carved on a separate block.

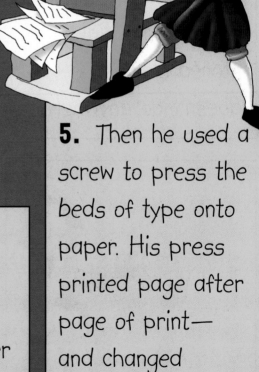

5. Then he used a screw to press the beds of type onto paper. His press printed page after page of print—and changed the world!

4. Gutenberg wanted a machine that would copy many pages all at once. So he first developed blocks of type that could be fitted together on a single plate, called a "bed."

Electric Letters

1. Samuel Morse loved painting as a hobby, but he needed to make money. His other interest was electricity. He decided to invent something using his knowledge. He wanted to see how electricity could be used to send information.

2. He knew you could store electricity in a battery. But stored electricity doesn't go anywhere.

3. He wanted to be able to move electricity from one place to another. He hoped to use electricity to carry signals from place to place. These signals could be used to form messages.

4. Morse believed he could send an electric signal along a wire. He invented a code of dots and dashes that could be made into long and short bursts of electricity.

5. The coded message could be tapped into an electric machine by the sender, to appear as dots and dashes on a paper tape for the receiver.

The Telegraph

The telegraph is an electric device that can send signal messages over a long distance.

The Morse Code

The telegraph uses bursts of electricity along a wire. Samuel Morse developed a code that translated the bursts of electricity into a series of dots and dashes. A short burst was a dot. A long burst was a dash. The message appeared on paper as a series of dots and dashes that made up letters of the alphabet. The most famous signal was the distress signal ...---... (SOS). This was the easiest signal to understand in an emergency.

Morse code tapper

17

The Telephone

A telephone is a machine that is able to send sound over long distances.

Alexander Graham Bell invented his telephone to make long-distance communication easier. He knew sound traveled in waves. He also knew the waves could make things vibrate.

What he wanted to do was make the vibrations work with electricity. His machine, the first telephone, changed sound vibrations into electric pulses.

Telephone Network

As the telephone became popular, a network of switching centers was set up to connect all the customers to each other.

1. As a young boy, Alexander Graham Bell was educated mostly at home. Later, he followed in his father's footsteps and became a teacher.

2. As a teacher, he worked with deaf people, helping them communicate. He experimented with sound as he taught deaf children to speak.

Sounds Along a Wire

3. He wanted to know if it was possible to **transmit** sound using some kind of machine. He became very interested in sound and how it worked.

4. He discovered that sound traveled along in waves, and that these sound waves caused vibrations. Perhaps a machine could work using vibrations, too.

5. He teamed up with Thomas Watson, who was a good mechanic. Together they invented a machine that had a soft iron flap that vibrated when electricity was passed through it. Using this machine, sound vibrations could be changed into electric pulses. The pulses passed up and down wires. With a machine at each end of the wire, sounds could be turned into pulses and back to sounds again!

On the Radio

Broadcasting means sending out signals that can be received by a radio or television. Before radio, no one had ever heard a broadcast. It was the beginning of a new age of communication.

Radio Is Born

In 1864, scientist James Maxwell predicted that an electrical spark, or signal, would produce an invisible wave. He was right! In the early 1900s, Guglielmo Marconi made this theory work, sending a certain kind of invisible wave—a radio wave—farther and farther, and finally across the Atlantic Ocean!

Radio Waves

Radio waves turned out to belong to the same family as light waves—except you can't see radio waves. Where you are right now, there are probably hundreds of radio waves moving past you in all directions!

Radio

A "radio" is actually a radio wave receiver. Inside is an aerial that picks up the radio waves and changes them into electricity and then into sound.

A radio DJ selects music to be changed into electric pulses. An aerial, or antenna, changes them into radio waves and broadcasts the waves from the radio station.

Radios in the 1930s and 1940s were powered by huge batteries, so they were big and heavy. They looked more like pieces of furniture.

A tiny device called a transistor changed things. Now radios could be much smaller—even pocket-sized!

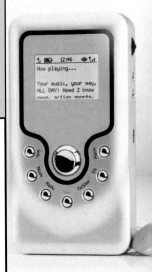

Today's radios are run by **microchips**.

Moving Pictures

When the camera was invented, people loved using it to take photographs and record the events, places, and people in their lives. But photographers soon wanted to move on—to make pictures that would move.

Moving pictures that you see as films are really lots of still pictures that follow one another very quickly. They move so fast, they fool your brain into thinking the picture is moving.

Movies

The Lumiere brothers opened the first movie theater in 1895. Their projector made the images larger when they were projected onto a screen. The first movies had no sound. They were "silent" films. Then "talkies" came along, and in the late 1920s the first color movies were seen.

Baird's Set

John Logie Baird made the first television in 1926. It was made of spinning glass, a hat box, and old cans, among other things!

A better TV, using a cathode ray tube and electron gun, was invented in 1953.

Television Broadcasting

A television is a machine for receiving sounds and pictures sent from a broadcaster. The signal is transmitted over the air on radio waves or through a cable. Television can show news and events as they actually happen as well as recorded programs. In a TV studio, cameras and microphones change pictures and sound into electrical signals. These are then changed into the signals that are transmitted to TVs.

Chemical TV

An electron is a tiny speck of matter that spins around the nucleus of an atom. In a cathode ray tube, electron guns shoot very sharp beams of electrons at a special screen. Chemicals in the screen glow when the electrons hit them.

There are three electron guns, one for each of three chemicals in the screen. The three chemicals glow red, green, and blue to make up the image.

Digital flat-screen **LCD** and plasma televisions are now replacing cathode ray tube televisions.

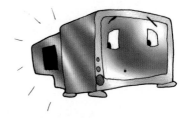

Braille and Hand Signals

People have been using sign language for thousands of years, but signs are of no use to someone who is blind. In 1824, a French man named Louis Braille developed a system that allowed blind people to read and write. It used patterns of six raised dots as an alphabet that could be felt.

When Louis Braille was three years old, he had a terrible accident. He stabbed himself in the eye with a sharp tool. His other eye became infected and Louis became blind. He was sent to a school for the blind in Paris where the students had to live on bread and water.

Some time later, a soldier named Barbier told Louis of a code he dreamed up to help soldiers send messages in the dark. Louis decided to develop this for a new use. His code, called Braille, worked well. It is now used by blind people everywhere.

Signing

Sign languages use facial expressions and hand signals to stand for words and images, so that deaf people can make themselves understood.

Even babies can learn a very simple sign language before they learn to talk and can let people know what they need or how they are feeling!

25

Radar

Radar is a special kind of communication. It's a way of finding out where objects are when you can't actually see them. Radar can also be used to direct war missiles to a target.

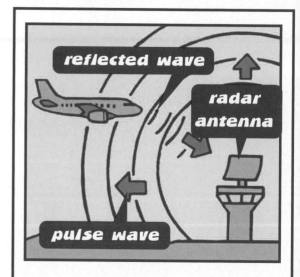

When a **pulse wave** shoots out from the radar set, it bounces off its target and heads back. The returning wave hits the antenna, and the receiver unit causes a "bleep" to show on the radar screen.

A radar set sends out radio waves. These bounce off an object like a ball bounces off a wall. The bounced waves return and cause a bleep on the receiving screen of the radar set. A map on the screen shows where the object is located.

During World War II, radar helped fighters find and shoot down enemy bombers.

Who Invented Radar?

Radar was first used in 1935 by a Scottish scientist named Robert Watson-Watt. U.S. and German researchers were also working on the idea. But, in nature, bats use a kind of radar to avoid bumping into things. So no one actually "invented" radar.

Sonar Systems

Sonar systems are similar to radar systems, except that they are used to detect objects, like submarines, underwater. They use sound waves instead of radio waves.

Phased-Array Radar

This is the kind of radar used by high-tech guided missiles to guide them to their target. The system uses a transmitter and receiver on the ground and a radar antenna in the missile. When the radar detects a target, a computer decides when to launch the missile. The radar then tracks both target and missile until they hit. Phased-array radar is also used to track weather systems.

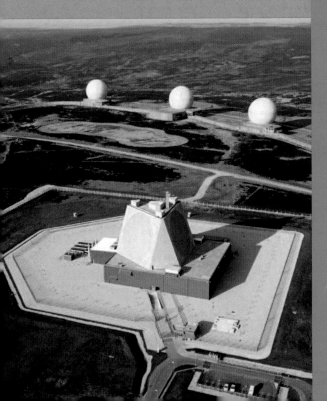

The Internet

Who would have thought, not so long ago, that we'd be able to talk to people all over the world with our computers? Now we can, thanks to the World Wide Web and Internet.

During the 1960s, the U. S. Army's Advanced Research Projects Agency, or ARPA, began working on developing a network of computers that could "talk" to each other.

By 1969, they created a network of four computers in different universities that could do this. It was called the ARPAnet.

Soon more networks were set up, and they all merged with the ARPAnet to create a huge super-network. It was called the interconnected network of networks, or the Internet.

Tim Berners-Lee invented a software program that allowed pictures and moving images to be sent on the Internet—the World Wide Web.

The World Wide Web

Now the World Wide Web is part of the computer network called the Internet. It's like a giant encyclopedia providing text, sound, pictures, and moving images.

Web Sites

The Web is made up of electronic addresses called web sites. Each one contains web pages. These hold multimedia information and are stored in computers connected to the Internet.

The Web has multimedia capabilities. That means it can be used for graphics, audio, and video. It makes the Internet a very useful communication tool.

New Industries

As a new, modern communication system, the Internet has led to the development of new industries, such as web-page design and computer games!

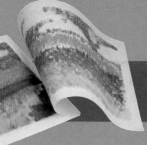

Communications Quiz

1. What were papyrus scrolls made from?

2. Who invented a code to be sent along telegraph wires?

3. Who invented beds of type blocks that made printing much faster?

4. What device allowed bombers to be spotted before they reached their target?

5. Which device for sending sound over long distances did Alexander Graham Bell invent?

6. What did Guglielmo Marconi send across the Atlantic Ocean?

7. Who made the first television in 1926?

8. Who invented an alphabet you can feel?

9. What type of gun shoots at a television screen?

10. What was the earliest kind of book with "pages" called?

1. A water plant 2. Samuel Morse 3. Johannes Gutenberg 4. Radar 5. The telephone 6. Radio waves 7. John Logie Baird 8. Louis Braille 9. An electron gun 10. A codex

Glossary

bookkeeping: recording and keeping track of financial (money) activities

LCD: Liquid Crystal Display; a way of showing readings on a screen using chemicals that show up in certain kinds of light and when a certain amount of electricity is applied to the screen

microchips: tiny pieces of material that will conduct electricity, store information, and help run computers and other electronic equipment

mold: a hollow structure or form that gives shape to something that is poured into it and allowed to harden

pulse wave: an electromagnetic or sound wave that lasts only a short length of time

scribes: scholars or people who copy documents

scrolls: rolls of paper or other material on which something has been written or engraved

sequence: a connected series of events, numbers, or objects; the order in which something happens

sonar: a system using sound waves to detect submarines or other objects underwater

sound waves: waves that are produced when a sound is made and is responsible for carrying the sound to the ear

transmit: to send a signal by radio waves or through a wire

Index